MEG'S CAR

D1514659

for Thomas

MEG'S CAR

by Helen Nicoll
and Jan Pieńkowski

PUFFIN BOOKS

It was a lovely day
for a picnic

Meg Mog and Owl
wanted to go
in a car

So Meg made a spell

Boot and bonnet
Rattle and clang
Make me a car
That goes with a bang

They
all
piled
into
the
new
car

Mog
started
the
engine

The car shot backwards

It went with a bolt and a jolt

a thump, a bump and a jump

The car started

It took off,

in a
tree

So they went to the picnic
on the broomstick

Goodbye!